AMHERST JR.
HIGH LIBRARY

The Wrestling Match

Amherst Regional Middle School
170 Chestnut Street
Amherst, MA 01002

D1510815

Also by Buchi Emecheta

Children's Fiction
The Moonlight Bride

Novels
In the Ditch
Second-Class Citizen
The Slave Girl
The Bride Price
The Joys of Motherhood

AMHERST JR.
HIGH LIBRARY

The Wrestling Match

BUCHI EMECHETA

George Braziller • New York

F
Eme

Published in the United States in 1983 by George Braziller, Inc.

Originally published in Great Britain by Oxford University Press in association with University Press Limited, Oxford House, Iddo Gate PMB 5095, Ibadan, Nigeria

© Copyright Oxford University Press, 1980

All rights reserved.
For information address the publisher:
George Braziller, Inc.
One Park Avenue
New York, NY 10016

Library of Congress Cataloging in Publication Data
Emecheta, Buchi.
   The wrestling match.

   Summary: Sixteen-year-old Okei, left an orphan after the Nigerian civil war, engages in a wrestling match to prove to his critical uncle and aunt that he is not as idle and worthless as they think.
   [1. Nigeria—Fiction]   I. Title.
PZ7.E575Wr   1983   [Fic]   82-17750
ISBN 0-8076-1060-7
ISBN 0-8076-1061-5 (pbk.)

It was during that quiet part of the evening when all the buyers and sellers of the Eke market had gone home. It was not yet time for the noises of children playing in the moonlight to be heard; they were all on the mud verandahs around their thatched huts, eating their evening meal. It was the time for the swishes of the fronds of the coconut-palms to be heard; it was the time for the fire-insects of the night to hiss through the still air. It was the time for the frogs in the nearby ponds to croak to their mates, as if to say that they should now seek shelter because night was fast approaching.

But this quiet did not last long. In the compound of Obi Agiliga, his senior wife Nne Ojo was already murmuring. Soon the murmuring exploded into an outcry. 'Look,' she shouted, holding a piece of pounded yam she was about to swallow. 'Look, if you are not satisfied with the best your family can do for you, go and live elsewhere. I don't care what anybody says. I am doing my best with you. If you are not satisfied . . . .'

'Now what is all that noise about? Not Okei again?' thundered Obi Agiliga, struggling into his outer otuogwu cloth and seething with anger. 'What am I going to do about you? I did not ask those federal soldiers to kill your parents. I have told you this so many times. Are you the only boy who had lost his parents during the civil war?'

A young figure uncurled himself from the verandah where he had been sitting and eating with the others. He got up slowly, taking his time and almost stepping on the bowls of fish soup that stood on the mud floor. He extracted himself from the family, and was about to walk out of the compound when he changed his mind and said insultingly: 'Oh, Uncle, we have heard that before. Why don't you think of something new to say?'

Obi Agiliga's wife could take no more. 'You dare insult your father like that, you ungrateful boy? Every evening you have to eat badly, wading your dirty fingers in the soup-bowl as if you provided the food. If you don't stop this attitude, I will get boys of your age to beat you up.'

'Boys of my age . . . ha, I'd like to see you do that!'

Nne Ojo was a quick-tempered woman. She threw the pounded yam she had been rolling in her hand on to Okei's shoulder. And he laughed again in derision.

'The way he behaves, one would have thought that I have never been young before,' Obi Agiliga said, going back to his disrupted meal. 'Go and find something to do. Go with us to the farm, or even try and catch those friends of yours who have been stealing things from old people, or go and fight a wrestling match. Do anything to prove that you're a man, Okei. Not sit here arguing over soup with my wives. Go and be a man, just as I was when I was your age.'

'Yeah, wl.en I was your age, when I was your age. . . . I was not there to prove your claim, was I . . . when I was your age . . . .'

He strolled out of the compound with the angry voices of his uncle's wives still cutting the night air.

Immediately outside his uncle's compound, Okei was greeted with an easy laughter from two of his friends. They had been outside the compound waiting for him to finish his evening meal.

'The usual night song, I see,' remarked Nduka. He was sixteen years old, the same age as Okei; but whilst Okei was thin and lanky, Nduka was stocky and short. He had a very sharp tongue as well. Okei was not given to much talking, but when he lost his temper he really lost it.

The third boy, Uche, was nicknamed Mbekwu—the easy-going tortoise. He had the irritating habit of laughing at everything and at everybody. He was a year younger than the other two, but they all belonged to the same age-group, Umu aya Biafra: babies born around the civil war.

The ripple of the great civil war started around 1964 and culminated in the creation of a new nation of Biafra in May 1967. But the children born at the very beginning of the political deadlock, and all those born during the war, and those born towards the end of the war were all called Umu aya Biafra, because it was the greatest happening that had ever occurred in Nigeria. It was a civil war, which started among the politicians; the army stepped in to keep the peace, then the military leaders started to quarrel among themselves, and one created a new state, taking his followers with him. That state was Biafra. It was a civil war that did cost Nigeria dear. Almost a million lives were lost, not just on the losing side; those who won the war lost thousands of people too—showing that in any war, however justified its cause, nobody wins.

But that was a long time ago. Now Uche was giggling at Okei's anger. The other two simply ignored him and went on talking as if he was not there.

'Did you hear what my uncle was saying—that some

members of our age-group were stealing from old people? That cannot be true, can it?'

'Trouble with these old men is that they say things simply to hurt, without any proof,' Nduka said, watching a group of children coming out of their huts into the open air to play.

'I don't know, but he has been saying this for the past few market days, and it's becoming boring. I hope they don't think I am one of the thieves!'

'Yes, that is the trouble. If a member of our age-group steals, the adults will say that we all steal. And what annoys me is that the thief gets all the attention and publicity and we get nothing.'

'We get the nagging to go to the farm, to prove our manhood,' laughed Uche.

'You won't prove your manhood like that when you laugh and eat all the time like a woman,' snapped Okei. 'This is not a laughing matter. I wish I knew what to do. I sometimes wish I hadn't gone out into the back yard when these soldiers came and killed my family. Sometimes I wish I had died with them. Listening to these women every evening . . . hm . . . I'm getting really fed up with life.'

'Oh come on!' said Nduka. 'Life is only just beginning for us. It's not as bad as that. We've called on you to go to Akpei with us, to meet Josephine and her friends. They are on their way from the market there.'

'You're really crazy about this girl, aren't you, Nduka?'

Nduka shrugged his shoulders. 'Well, what else is there for me to do? Sit on our verandah and listen to my father telling me that I am hopeless, and that since my elder brother has been killed in the army there's no hope for our family line any more?'

'Does your father say that to you too?' Okei asked, incredulous.

Uche started to laugh uncontrollably.

'What have I said to make you go mad like that? One of

4

these days I'm going to show you that I don't like people who laugh when others are trying to be serious.'

'There is nothing to be serious about. You think you are the only one being nagged at? Well, you are wrong. The only good boys of our age-group are those who did not go to school at all—you know, who've been going to the farm with their parents all the four market days of the week—all through Eke, Olie, Nkwo, and Afo, and back again on another Eke day—since they took their first steps, and who will remain like that until their dying day. Those of us who went to school are no good.'

'Come on, let's go and meet the girls,' said Nduka, finishing the argument. 'At least they will be happy to see us.'

And they trotted into the darkening night on their way to Akpei.

2

By the time Okei and his friends got to the little hill that
bordered the Oboshi stream, the moon had risen full and
clear. It illuminated the sands, highlighting their silvery
colour the more. The silver path through which the boys
walked was thickly edged by dense evergreen bushes. Here
they came to a clearing in which there was a cluster of
cottages, most of them thatched but one or two roofed with
corrugated iron sheets that glistened in the moonlight.
There was an open clearing in which children and old
people sat, telling stories and singing by the moonlight.
The night was airy, and the young people on their way to
Akpei enjoyed the feel of it all. There was no need for much
conversation.

'We will have to run down the slope to the stream. I
always enjoy doing that,' Uche announced.

'Everybody enjoys that,' Okei cut in. 'I'll like to see you
run up on your way back.'

'You can't run up, though,' Nduka compromised,
'because in most cases you're carrying something from the
market or the stream.'

'Wait a minute. Why is it that Josephine and her friends had to go to Akpei to sell plantain on an Eke day, when there is a big market here in Igbuno?' asked Okei.

'You don't know our girls, you don't know them at all,' Nduka said, looking wise. 'They claim that in Akpei people are willing to pay more and that they are nicer.'

'So they walk all these miles for a few kobos?'

'Well,' Uche put in, 'going to meet them at least gives us something to do. Isn't that what the adults have been accusing us of? That we are idle?' And he got ready to run down the slope.

'Hm . . . maybe you are right, Uche,' said Okei. 'But I am going to Akpei this night to accompany a friend and age-mate, not to meet any silly, giggling girl.'

'So am I,' laughed Uche.

'All right, all right, it is my own fault. But you cannot deny that it is a lovely evening, too lovely to stay indoors or sit by old women listening to their old-fashioned stories. Let us run down. I am sure we shall not reach Akpei, because the girls will have left the market a long time ago.'

They tore down the slope, enjoying the wind whistling in their ears. At the bottom of the hill they all stopped short. They could hear voices. The voices of a group of girls.

'They are early. They must have left earlier than they normally do,' remarked Nduka.

'I know what's happened,' Okei said in a low voice. 'I think they have had a good market and sold their plantain very quickly. You did say that they are eager for Igbuno plantain in Akpei. Lazy people, the people of Akpei. Can't they grow their own plantain?'

'They are singing again,' laughed Uche.

'Sh . . . sh . . . we do not want them to know that we are here,' Nduka said. 'Otherwise they will not have their bath—and they won't thank us for that. So we just have to sit here quietly until they have finished washing, then we will surprise them with our presence.'

Nobody contradicted him. They all flopped themselves down by the low bush near the stream. They lay on their backs, watching the slow movements of the moon whilst the voices of the chattering girls reached them distinctly.

The girls splashed and sang as they washed themselves. Then a voice said clear and loud: 'You know, if I could afford it I would never go to Akpei again, not after today. Who do they think they are, that's what I'd like to know. They are playing the big people just because we take plantain to their villages. God, and their boys . . . aren't they annoying?'

'There is no smoke without fire, though. Maybe there is some truth in what they were saying.'

'Well, if their accusations were true, should they not go to our young men and say it to them face to face? Why make all these innuendoes . . . and to us? We did not mug their old people, we did not break into the houses of our elders. If all those things had happened at all, only boys could have done them. Our elders make sure we girls are too busy to have time for such things.'

'You know, the boys in our age-group are all capable of many things. Because they have been to school they do not wish to farm any more. And they are not educated enough to take up big jobs in the cities.'

'They can be houseboys, though.'

'Houseboys? These boys? Can you imagine a bighead like Okei being anybody's houseboy?'

There was a peal of laughter.

'Oh, I don't know. If there is any truth in all this, I won't be surprised if they were led by our Okei.'

The girls laughed again, and went on splashing so much water that their voices were drowned by the sheer noises of their movements.

'If I lay my hands on that girl . . .' Okei growled from where he was sitting. He had sat bolt upright when he heard his name mentioned.

8

'Please, Okei, don't do anything rash,' begged Nduka. 'They are only girls, and don't forget that they were told this by those young people from Akpei.'

'But why me? Why me? I have nothing to do with it. My uncle was making such insinuations earlier on. Why me?'

'Because, Okei, you are taller than any of us. You are more polished. You know, you were born into a little wealth and you started life richer than any of us. All that has given you the makings of a leader. So you are the uncontested leader of our age-group. You get blamed for things like this. I must talk to Josephine, though. She should watch her tongue.'

'You better make sure you do. As for those Akpei weak-livered boys, we will deal with them. What do old people have that I'd like to take? Some of them are so poor.'

'We can do something, though. We can arrange a meeting of all our age-group, and take it in turns to police the areas where these thieves operate,' Uche suggested, giggling at Okei's anger.

'But that's a good suggestion, Uche. Please don't spoil it by your stupid laughter. At least they will not accuse us of doing nothing. As for those people in Akpei . . . .'

'No,' Nduka said, 'leave those people until we all meet, then we will decide how to deal with them.'

The girls, with their wares delicately balanced on their heads, walked out of the stream still talking of this and that, until they saw Okei and his friends. They stopped short, not at first knowing what to do.

Josephine stepped forward in a brave attempt to cover their confusion. 'Have you been waiting here long?'

'No,' said Nduka hurriedly, 'we were just coming from the village. You must have left Akpei very early today, or we were late in leaving. You normally are not here by the time we meet you.'

'Yes, we sold our plantains very quickly today, didn't we?' her friends agreed, but one small girl started to laugh.

'And why do you want to know if we have been waiting here long or not?' growled Okei. 'Have you been saying sly things about us?'

'Oh, Okei!' shouted an elegant girl of seventeen, Kwutelu. She was the oldest of all the girls, the most sophisticated and the one that the others modelled their behaviour by. 'I didn't know you were here with the others! You are really beginning to care for us, coming to meet us on our way from Akpei. Thank you very much.'

'I did not come to meet you, Kwutelu. I only accompany my friend Nduka here,' Okei snarled. 'And am I so indistinct that you cannot see me in this clear moon?'

'Ahem, let us share your wares,' Nduka said quickly. 'Josephine, give me half of your things, I'll relieve you of the load.' The others stood there and watched enviously as Nduka took all the heavy things from Josephine's basket and slung them across his thick shoulder.

Uche, not to be left out, took bits from each of the other five girls. But Okei was unmoved by all this show of affection. He was hurt and he was angry. He was dying to know more about the gossip from Akpei, but pride would not let him ask the girls. And the girls did not wish to pursue the conversation. Some of them had a suspicion that they had been overheard.

As they walked home the girls concentrated on being girls, being nice and being feminine. They brought out the roasted cashew nuts they had bought, and distributed them among themselves. They sang, made light conversation, and laughed just as Igbuno girls were expected to do.

Okei did not say a word, amidst all this show.

They parted at the market square. 'You, Uche, go round and make the announcements. We must all meet tomorrow by the moonlight, in front of my uncle Obi Agiliga's compound,' Okei said as he walked away very quickly, leaving the group to wonder about him.

'I don't like that young man very much,' Kwutelu remarked.

'You don't have to like him. He does not go for girls like you,' Uche said, sniggering.

'And what type of girls does he go for?' snapped Kwutelu.

'College girls, not gossip market girls from Akpei market. Here, take your stuff, I am going home. The moon is waning too,' Uche said, half in joke and half in seriousness, confusing his listeners.

People never knew whether to take Uche seriously or not.

3

The sun was very high in the sky and the heat was almost unbearably intense. All the leaves along the footpaths drooped from lack of moisture. All the bush animals had sought for shelter in the shades of trees and the giant grass. Even the ever-chattering wood-parrots were silent. So hot was the afternoon. Obi Agiliga knew that it was time for him and his farm-hands to have a rest. It was time for him to go into the cool shed on his farm and lie on the beaten floor to smoke his pipe.

His paid helpers saw him and wordlessly followed his example. They all ambled into different parts of the bush in search of shelter.

'If only I could have more hands on this farm. Then I could be sure that all the yams would be harvested before the yam festival,' Obi Agiliga moaned as he stretched his tall body on the cool floor. 'Onuoha, go to the stream and get some water. We must have something to eat before we go on. This sun can burn life out of any man.'

'I'll be back in no time at all, Father,' said Onuoha, his

twelve-year-old son. 'Are you not happy about the progress of the harvesting?'

'Hmm, I am not too happy. When the sun is so hot it burns out all the moisture from the yams. So we will have to hurry.'

'I wish you could make Okei come to the farm sometimes to help. He is very strong, yet he does not like coming to the farm at all.'

'I know, but he is troubled about something, Onuoha. We don't know what it is. And he did not dream that he would ever be asked to come and work on the farm. That Awolowo free education has given him and his age-group airs. They will grow, never mind. They all will grow.'

Father and son stopped talking as they listened carefully, knowing that a group of people were approaching their shed. Onuoha peeped into the bush-path, and the fear and curiosity in his young face were transformed and became a trusting and joyous glow.

'Father, you have visitors. It's Obi Uwechue from Akpei. I must run to the stream to get you all something to drink.' So saying, he dashed into the bush-path, his young and determined feet crackling the dry fallen leaves as he went.

'It must be an important matter that brought you to my farm in this heat and at this time of year. Please sit down, sit down. The floor is cool at least.'

'The matter is very urgent indeed, my friend,' said Obi Uwechue. 'And I do not want to come to your compound, because the women would interfere. How is your family?'

They all sat down and distributed kola nuts, and drank some cool palm-wine which Obi Uwechue had brought. Onuoha soon arrived from the stream and, with the help of his father's helpers, made a bush-meat soup which they all ate with pounded yam. Obi Agiliga studied his visitor all the time, wondering why he had come at such an odd time. But he was soon relieved of his suspense.

'My friend, you have a troublesome age-group in your

village in Igbuno. We have the same in ours. I have never come across such stubborn young men. In Akpei it is now becoming difficult for women to walk down a footpath on moonless nights, a thing which we have never heard of before. Yesterday we had to send your girls away home early because they started picking quarrels with them. They say that your young men are equally bad. And of course a fight almost broke out. But during the argument, the name of your nephew was being mentioned all the time. . . .'

Obi Uwechue paused and looked around the farm hut, and laughed gently. 'I was even hoping that I might find him on your farm today, since it is harvest-time.'

'You are hoping for the moon, my friend,' Obi Agiliga replied. 'That boy is driving us all mad. And he is setting a very bad example for my younger sons. Onuoha here admires his strength. What shall we do, my friend? This must stop.'

'Last Nkwo day, for example, some of your boys came into our stream to fish, when they know quite well that it is forbidden. They did not just fish, they muddled all the cassava pulp which our women were soaking in the stream.'

'Funny, I did not hear of all this, and my nephew did not say a word,' Obi Agiliga remarked reflectively.

They were silent for a while, then as if on cue they both started to laugh. Obi Uwechue was the first one to speak.

'You remember what our fathers used to say, that when young men are idle the elders must give them something to worry about. I think we will have to create a big worry for our young men. By the time they have finished solving that problem they will be wiser.'

'I was thinking of the same thing. The girls will be very useful. Women always have sharp tongues. Encourage your girls to start talking . . . you know, making pungent songs . . . and leave the rest to me,' Obi Agiliga said with a knowing wink.

4

Uche got up very early the following morning and rushed to the stream. This was very unusual, and his family thought that maybe he was having a change of heart. They hoped that he would probably be going to the farm with the rest of the men in the family.

He ran down the slope leading to the stream, as usual, and looked uncertainly at the clear water as it tumbled over tiny rocks and then formed a deep pool at the bottom of the stream. There were very few people about, one or two early risers. He did not say anything to them. He stood there scowling at the water. It was a chilly morning, and the thought of dipping into the stream took some courage. He was feeling the water with his feet when he heard his friend and age-mate whistling as he ran down the slope.

'Ah,' sneered Nduka, 'someone is feeling the water like an old woman.'

'No I am not. I was only thinking,' replied Uche, holding his breath and ready for a compulsory plunge. He knew that if he did not get into the water by himself his friend would push him in, and he would laugh at him as well. So

15

before Nduka could reach him he threw his shorts on the nearby rocks and dashed into the water.

'You know I would have helped you to make up your mind,' laughed Nduka.

'Well, I have cheated you of your fun. You are early. Going to Akpei with your Josephine?'

'She is not my Josephine. She is just a friend. And people don't go to Akpei on Olie day. They go on Eke days to sell. I want to have my bath early in order to start the announcements for our gathering this night.'

'So do I,' Uche said. 'And look, I have a big gourd here to take home enough water to last my family the whole day. But they will not talk of that. They will only talk of the fact that I did not go to the farm.'

'Hmm, I would have gone to the farm today myself, but this gathering is more important to me. I am taking home a lot of water too.'

'Listen, Nduka, how are we going to make the announcements? Okei did not say . . . maybe he expects us to beat a drum. . . .' Uche started to laugh.

'Use whatever method you like, but make sure all our age-group in your area hear about it.'

'All our age-group—what of those who did not go to school, those who are playing at being good boys and go to the farms with their fathers? Should we not leave them out?'

Both boys did not know how to deal with this situation. Before their time, an age-group was an age-group. Now they had the educated ones and the uneducated ones. Should the uneducated ones be left out? Nduka was thinking of writing out the announcements for the meeting, instead of using a gong as people normally did. But if he wrote it out, would those of them who were illiterate get the message? He said reflectively: 'I think we better include them. If they feel they cannot understand us, then they can absent themselves.'

'Suppose we start speaking in English?' asked Uche, showing off.

'How many English words have you mastered? You are silly sometimes. Do you forget that we have many age-mates who are already in colleges? How would you feel if they exclude you in our age-gathering just because you stopped at Primary Six?'

Uche gobbled his morning meal and waited for his people to leave for the farm, before he ransacked his mother's hut for a gong. He was not going to write the announcement. Nduka was right. He did not command enough English language for such a task. He started to beat the gong.

'All the males belonging to the Umu aya Biafra age-group are to meet in front of Obi Agiliga's compound when the moon is out this evening. All the males belonging . . . .'

A group of girls going to the stream saw him and wondered what the troublesome age-group had got to say to each other. 'After all the trouble they have been causing. Go to your father's farm and help!' shouted one bold girl.

Uche ignored them and went on with his announcements. He would beat the gong three times to arrest attention, then deliver his message, and beat the gong three times more to emphasize the end of his announcement.

Nduka took up the other side of Igbuno. But he copied out his message in shaky, large letters and distributed them by hand. He had to use plain sheets from his old school exercise book, because the age-group did not have much money. If we claim to be educated we must do things the way educated people do their things, he said to himself in justification for his action.

Okei enlisted the help of the young children in his uncle's compound and they swept the front of the compound leading to the footpath.

He was quiet and sullen, and the wives in the compound knew that something was on his mind. They teased him into anger, knowing that he would explode at the least provocation, but he seemed unaware of them. He was the more determined not to argue with anybody, when he noticed that his uncle Obi Agiliga was staying longer than usual on the farm.

'The Obi must be working so hard today. It is always like this during yam harvest time. Poor Obi. So much work,' his senior wife Nne Ojo remarked pointedly.

The other, younger wives agreed, and all expressed the view that another pair of male hands would have been such a welcome gift to Obi Agiliga.

Okei knew that they were referring to his pair of idle hands. But he said nothing. If he picked up quarrel with any of them, the story would be repeated differently to his absent uncle.

By the time they had finished their evening meal many of the young people were already gathering. The meeting soon started.

Just as Okei had expected, he was elected as the leader of the age-group. Even though he himself doubted whether he had been a good choice, yet the cheers with which the election was greeted showed him that his age-mates had confidence in him. They went through all the allegations that had been blamed on them, and nobody seemed to have done any of them. But towards the tail-end Uche, of all people, got up. He coughed and twiddled his ears for a time and then confessed:

'I got so fed up with all the lies told about us that last Nkwo day I went to Akpei to fish. Well, I must give them something to talk about. I did that on purpose with three of my younger half-brothers. It will not happen again.'

'To think that you of all people should do a thing like that,' Okei shouted. 'Were you very hungry? Can't your father feed you? You disgrace us. Does the group think we have to punish him?'

'No,' was the unanimous answer.

'He is silly and he has promised not to do so again. I will keep an eye on him,' finished Nduka.

It was then decided that all the other insults heaped upon them from the young people of Akpei would be settled in a wrestling match. 'It will be a friendly one, just like a play, but it will settle our superiority once and for all,' Okei said.

This was greeted cheerfully too.

The match would be played strictly according to the wrestling rules. They would select their best wrestlers, and the Akpei young people would select theirs. They would not invite the elders from the two villages to decide the better of the two. The young men of Igbuno were quite sure of their winning, because they felt they had been wrongly accused.

'How come they started to accuse us in the first place?' asked Nduka.

'Because they hear our elders talking of our faults in the open, washing our dirty linen outside under the very noses of those chicken-livered Akpei boys,' explained one farmer's boy from Obi Ogbeukwu's compound. 'Never mind, we will teach them, we will teach them.'

Well, he talked sense, thought Okei as he sat there on the silvery sand, watching his friends. To think that that farmer's boy never spent a day in school. Aloud he said: 'But what are we going to do about this farming business?'

'How can we farm using the old, old method which our great-great-grandparents had used?' Nduka said. 'Look at our fathers. They spend four days out of every five, from sunrise to sundown on the farm. What do they have to show for it? Only enough yams to feed each family, and during dry season we almost starve. And what do we get from yams? Only starch. They taught us this much at school. I am not going to throw my life away working on such a farm. I am still thinking of a way of avoiding it, if I am to stay in this village and be a farmer. I think we should let the elders know this.' He heaved his hefty chest in anger.

And he too was cheered. But the boys who had never been to school did not know what their friends and age-mates were saying. They knew their limitations though, so they cheered with the rest.

It was amidst this cheering and comradeship that Obi Agiliga came from his farm, tired out after such a long day. 'What is happening in front of my compound?' he roared. 'Clear out, all of you lazy lot! Clear out, you lazy, good-for-nothing pilferers of fishes and muggers of the old. . . .'

'Come in, come in, come in!' begged his senior wife, Nne Ojo. 'The Umu Biafra age-group are holding a meeting in front of your compound, that is all.' Here she laughed a little. 'Our future leaders and town planners . . . .'

Obi Agiliga allowed himself to be led in, and said in a low voice: 'They should think of how to fill their bellies first. I must eat quickly. I have a word or two to say to the elders of Igbuno. This state of affairs must not go on.'

The young people hurried over their deliberations and dispersed noisily. Okei and Nduka were to practise their wrestling skills, and the farmer's boy from Ogbeukwu was to go to Akpei the following day and throw the challenge to the loud mouths from Akpei.

'We will show them,' Okei boasted in encouragement. 'The wrestling match will decide who was in the wrong, and it will settle all the bickering and gossips once and for all.'

Much later that evening Obi Agiliga went to see a few friends in their compound. He returned very late, when the moon was so clear and the footpaths so silent that the whole area looked like man-made glass. The air was so cool and light, the trees so clear in their thickness, that one was tempted to stay outside. But a mischievous smile played on the sealed lips of Obi Agiliga.

'These boys thought they were the only people who have ever been young. They will learn, sure they will learn,' he murmured as he made his way to his own compound.

5

Okei, at the age of sixteen, knew what was expected of him as a leader. He worried over it most of the night, but there was one thing he was determined on: the leadership was not going to be taken from him. He had been told stories of failed leaders when he was very little. Such ideas were woven into the native fables told to children by their grannies on moonlight nights. He was going to be a good leader, and would live up to the expectations of those who had elected him.

He got up early the next day. He ran up and down the incline that led to the stream, in order to toughen his feet. He knew that as a result of this kind of exercise his feet would not give way easily for his opponent to fell him in wrestling.

'Ah, you have started already?' greeted Nduka, who had come to the spot for his toughening-up and practising with Okei.

'Yes, I have to do this part of it early to avoid the curious,' Okei said as he panted.

'Oh, we can never prevent them from asking questions.

AMHERST JR.
HIGH LIBRARY

Did you tell your uncle—I mean your little father, as you
are expected to say—that you have been elected the leader
of your age-group?'

'No. Whatever for? It won't interest him.'

'I am sure it will. They say he was a great wrestler during
his time.'

'He never lets us forget it.'

They ran up and down the slope many more times, until
they were completely exhausted. Okei flopped on the nearby
low bush, breathing hard. 'I think all our age-group should
toughen themselves up. You never know. I may lose the
fight, and it could become an open one.'

'There are rules to these wrestling matches, you know,'
Nduka said. 'In any case, all our age-mates do wrestle for
fun in their different compounds.'

'That may be so, but I still would like it to become the
accepted thing. They should all practise, not just the two of
us.'

'Ah, you are now talking as a leader,' laughed Nduka.

'You all nominated me . . . . Come on, let us wrestle.'

They moved to a sandier area and started to practise their
wrestling. They both sweated profusely. People on their way
to the stream soon started to pass them. Some gave them
their praise-names in form of greetings, others just stared,
encouraging this one against that one. It was all done in a
lighthearted mood. The people of Igbuno loved such sports.

Soon a lighter, noisier group was approaching them. The
wrestlers could tell that they were young people by the
sounds their water-cans made against their carrier trays.
They knew that they were girls. Then the approaching
crowd saw them and stopped.

'Should we stop wrestling?' Nduka asked, uncertain.

'But why? They are going to the stream and we are
wrestling. Just ignore them,' Okei admonished his friend
hoarsely.

But the two young men could see from the corner of their

eyes that the girls were led by Kwutelu, and they both knew that she could be very provoking. They saw that she started to whisper something to the other girls, and this unnerved the wrestlers.

Then all of a sudden the girls burst out laughing. Kwutelu covered her mouth in amusement, and walked on her toes in an annoying manner towards Okei and Nduka.

'Oh, so you are wrestling?' she asked in suppressed laughter.

'What is bad in wrestling? Or are you frightened we might floor your friends from Akpei?' Nduka snapped.

'Why don't you keep quiet, for God's sake?' Okei shouted at his friend. But Nduka was not the one to be silenced. He cared for and respected Josephine, but not that arrogant Kwutelu. He did not hate her, only he did not so much as care for her.

'Why should we let her get away with her saucy remarks? Yes, we are practising in order to challenge your friends from Akpei. Go and tell them. Come on, let's go, Okei. We've had enough for one morning anyway.'

'Oh . . . so all this ballyhoo is for the Akpei boys,' Kwutelu said. 'Do you want to hear more of what they have been saying? They said you even pinch little sprats from their streams, and steal from our old people.' She looked in amusement towards the other girls, who were laughing at it all and encouraging her.

'Look, enough is enough, do you hear me?' Okei said menacingly. 'Stop that nonsense. You know that there is no truth in all that. If you were a boy you wouldn't stand there saying all that to us. You are hiding behind the fact that you are a girl. But don't annoy me, because I can still beat girls up.' He was showing his anger now. He was very tired from their early practice, and that made him rather vulnerable.

'So you have now come so low as to talk to ordinary girls like us? I thought you go for college girls. And how come you are wrestling? I thought you have become too civilized for that, Okei the son of Agiliga.'

'There is no need in replying to you,' Nduka said. 'If you have retained anything you learnt at school you will remember that every nation on earth wrestles, even the white people.'

'Well, that is nice to hear, but I hope you go and practise your prowess on the sneaking thieves that lurk in the bushes at night, and not on innocent boys from Akpei. After all, all they did was to complain about your stealing fish from their stream . . . .'

'I wish I knew who the thieves were. And if I did, I would encourage them to come and burgle your father's compound. And that, I think, would put your poisonous tongue in check.'

'Oh, Okei, so you are threatening our compound now? You try it. My father will wait for you. And as for you and the boys from Akpei, you know what they say in our native fables, that the guilty person always loses in such an open fight. So you have to practise hard, to prove your innocence.'

Okei made a move toward her, but Nduka held him back. 'They will go and say that we are waylaying innocent girls. Don't do it, let us go.'

Then the girls burst into a song:

'Umu aya Biafra.
Stealer of sprats from the streams,
Molester of innocent girls by the streams,
They will never go to the farms,
They will never help in the house.
Akpei boys will teach them a lesson, a lesson . . . .'

Okei was so angry that he did not bother to go to the stream to wash himself. He simply walked home with his friend, hoping to go back to the stream later on.

'Who is going to marry that chatterbox of a girl, Kwutelu?' he asked all of sudden.

'I don't know him personally. They say he is on government service in Ilorin, one of the Yoruba towns in the west.'

'God help that man.'

Nduka laughed. 'I know what you mean. I wonder why she is going out of her way to annoy us, as if she had been set up into doing it. She was going to goad you into fighting her, and you know what that means. Her future parents-in-law and her real parents and their families would all go against us. That was why I was holding you.'

'Thank you. But I will teach her a lesson one of these days if she continues this way. I don't think she was set up against us. I have never heard that girl utter a polite word to anybody.'

'She is always cheeky, but not this far,' Nduka maintained.

6

As soon as Kwutelu got home from the stream, she felt it was her business to go and tell her friend Josephine all that had happened. Josephine did not go to the stream that early because she had to help in getting ready bits and pieces for the labourers who were going to help her father harvest the yams.

'This is the part of yam festivals that I hate most,' she moaned to Kwutelu. 'But how come you are not doing some work in your compound?'

'I am supposed to be claying the huts really, and my mother thought I was out in one of the groves getting the claying things. But I've just come to tell you this.'

She went into a great detail of all that took place that morning. How she had successfully ruffled Okei's feathers; how he was so angry that he almost struck her. But thank goodness, Nduka was there to hold him back. She told Josephine how amused they were and how they had laughed. 'Do you know, they really want to beat the Akpei boys in wrestling. What a big fun we are going to have watching them. Was it not a good thing that we started talking about it, eh?'

'I don't know, Kwutelu, if I like it all so much. I heard from my father this morning that they, the Umu Biafra, had a meeting last night. And the stupid boys had it in the open, and all the Agiliga household heard their deliberations.'

'I did not hear that one. What have they decided to do? Kill us all on our sleeping-mats?'

'Oh, Kwutelu, you tend to dramatize everything. They are only going to wrestle with the boys from Akpei, and I heard my father saying that things were changing. He said that during his time young boys came of age with dancing and songs, but this group are coming of age with wrestling.'

'Well, wrestling is a kind of sport, just like football the college boys play. At least Okei told me that much, this morning.'

'Hm, if it is taken to be a friendly sport it will be nice. But this one is starting with a gossip. I wish we did not start it, Kwutelu. That boy Okei is very intense.'

'Did your father tell you that we have done wrong?' Kwutelu asked.

'No, that's the funny part of it. I think the elders want us to goad them into anger. If you ask me, the elders from Akpei are doing the same,' Josephine said reflectively.

They both laughed, and agreed that it could not be true. Though they would like some of those proud Igbuno boys, who thought they were going to be young for ever, taught a lesson.

'I am glad Okei did not beat you up. That would have been bad for you.'

'And for him too.'

When Kwutelu's father, Obi Uju, returned from the farm, his pet daughter Kwutelu told him of Okei's threats. Her father became angry and asked. 'Can't our girls go to the stream without being molested? I must see his uncle

Obi Agiliga. If he has to tie that nephew of his with a string to his door-post, I am going to make sure that I make him do so. If he wishes to practise wrestling, why choose the pathway to the stream, just to be seen by everybody? If he threatens you again, just let me know. Since when have we stopped young girls from singing provoking songs? Is that not what women are made for, to provoke men? I don't understand these young people any more.'

Obi Uju did not feel like going out that evening. Few callers came to see him, and after they had all gone he felt he would retire early. He would have to get up early the following day to go and work on his farm with the few paid labourers he could afford. Labourers, especially paid ones, would look for any reason to dodge the work they were paid to do. The master had to be on the alert all the time. He must work hard himself, setting a good example. This was even more imperative with Obi Uju, because he could only get three workers and could only afford to pay them for four days. Four days, which he calculated would be just enough to finish the toughest part of his harvesting. He must make sure the workers worked for every kobo he paid them. He called his daughter to fill his evening pipe for him.

'You are retiring early,' Kwutelu remarked indulgently. She was well loved by her father. She was always close to him, and he spoilt her. Many of Obi Uju's youngest wives resented this, but they all now took consolation in that she would be going away to her husband soon after the yam festival. Meanwhile Kwutelu knew that she was free to sleep in her father's sleeping-house or her mother's hut. Her father's house had spare inner rooms. She liked these better than her mother's thatched hut. When teased about it she used to say: 'I like sleeping under corrugated iron sheets.' Her listeners would smile indulgently, knowing full well that her future husband worked as a sales manager in one of the Nigerian companies in Ilorin.

She filled the pipe for her father, and with the youngest

wife in the family swept and got ready his sleeping-place. Clean goatskins were spread on a wooden bed and a feather-filled pillow was placed on a wooden headrest.

'I think you have guests,' the young wife told Kwutelu.

'Oh,' she gasped as she listened to the noises that were coming into the inner room from the compound. 'Yes, you are right. I can hear my future brothers-in-law whistling. I must go. I will entertain them in the compound. Father is too tired tonight to receive any more guests.'

'Yes, he is dozing already. These harvests, they are men-killers.'

'I know,' Kwutelu said as she made her way out into the compound. She glanced at her father on her way and said casually: 'I am in the compound, father, if you want anything.'

'No, daughter, go and be nice to your future brothers. They are growing impatient, I can tell by the wonkiness of their whistle.'

Kwutelu laughed lightly as she dashed out to welcome her fiancé's brothers. They were happy to see her. They had heard that Okei had waylaid her on her way to the stream, and had come to find out why. Kwutelu told them all that happened in a lighthearted way, because she did not wish to start trouble for her future in-laws. That, she knew, would give her a bad name. They were both farmers, very traditional, and would take no nonsense from anybody. By the time she had finished her story they were all laughing at the naïvety of the young people born around the civil war.

'They are so proud about being partly educated,' Kwutelu emphasized. 'They are like bats, neither birds nor animals. After all, people like your big brother were educated in this village. They did not burn our huts down.'

She went into her mother's hut and brought them some nuts. They all ate, and they talked and kept her company till the moon had really gone pale. They wished her goodnight, and warned her to be a good girl because she was already their wife. Kwutelu knew all that on the day her bride-price was paid. She promised to be good, and they saw her make her way to her father's house.

She did not like going to her mother's hut tonight, because she would wake up and tell her how late she was. Yes, all the young children playing outside had gone to sleep, but she was only chatting. She could hear her mother warning her against making herself cheap by over-exposure to her future in-laws, and these warnings had begun to get on her nerves. So she made her way to her father's sleeping-house. He would say nothing, nothing at all.

Obi Uju, Kwutelu's father, was deep in sleep, his tired body relaxed on the cool goatskins that had been lovingly laid out for him in his inner room by his daughter and youngest wife. He opened his eyes suddenly, not because the first bout of tiredness had ebbed away as a result of his retiring early but because he sensed that somebody was moving outside his outer door. He had got up earlier on, when it was very dark and when he guessed that his family were all asleep, and had hooked the heavy catch that held in the heavy wooden door. So he probably was dreaming.

Then he heard the sound again. This time he sat bolt upright. No, he was not dreaming. There was a determined rattling and pushing noise going on. The person was being careful not to wake the household. But for Obi Uju, whose well-trained ears were accustomed to hearing the slightest hiss of a snake, the noise at the door was loud enough. Then he remembered the threat Kwutelu told him that Okei had made to her earlier in the day.

'So, that stupid boy Okei thought he would carry out his threat? What is the world coming to? In the olden days one would have been justified in killing a thief like this one. But things have changed now. And I do not want to get involved in any unnecessary lawsuits over so silly a boy, and at this time of year too. But the boy must be taught a lesson, a lesson he will always remember for the rest of his life. He must learn never to defy and laugh at his elders. He must learn the fact that we, the older ones, have seen greater things happen than young people of his age.'

He got up and soundlessly padded his way to the shelf by his head and took out a small cutlass which he used for cutting young corn. He crept quietly towards the door. 'Sorry, son, that I have to teach you a lesson which you refused to learn from your uncle, and sorry that I have to teach you in this ghastly way. But you will live,' Obi Uju thought. 'This cutlass will scar you for life, but will not kill or break any bones of your body. To be threatened by such a tiny boy. What an insult!'

The pushing of the wooden door became stronger, and Obi Uju helped the thief outside by unhinging the door from the inside. The door gave way slightly with a whining noise.

The moon had waned, but the distinct shape of a young person's shoulder was visible in the dark. This fired the anger in Obi Uju's mind. 'To think that I am even older than your father . . . you threatening me . . . .' With that he aimed the cutlass at the shoulder, making sure to control the force with which it would land on the silly thief. The person outside instinctively dodged it, and instead of scratching the shoulder-blade as Obi Uju had calculated, it landed on the side of the head, cutting a young ear neatly off.

Then a scream rang out, piercing and painful like that of a goat being killed. 'Oh, Father . . . Father . . . why do you want to kill me? Father, it's only me, your daughter Kwutelu.'

Obi Uju dropped the knife, looked at his own hands, and then stretched them both out to catch the sagging body of his beloved daughter before she hit the hard floor.

Then he took up the cry, but his was heavy with anguish and bitterness. 'Wake up, wake up, everybody. Come and see the abomination, an abomination which has never happened in our village. I have killed my own daughter, with my own hands, all because of Umu aya Biafra. Wake up, wake up . . . an abomination . . . an abomination . . . .'

7

The cry of 'Umu aya Biafra, Umu aya Biafra' echoed from one end of Igbuno to the other. The cries cut through the otherwise still night like the sharp edges of so many shooting swords. The sounds seemed to give even the very still, dark leaves of trees bordering every footpath and open place a life of their own. They all seemed to quiver with the intensity of it all.

At first all the members of Obi Agiliga's compound were justly sleeping like everybody else. Obi Agiliga's house was in the innermost part of the compound. His wives' huts were built on both sides, and the whole set of buildings was surrounded with thatched walls made of very young, strong palm-fronds. A big gate sealed the whole compound from the rest of the village.

Nne Ojo's hut was the first one on the right. Because she was the nearest to the gate, she was always the first to hear shouts and gong announcements.

On this night, she could not believe her ears. 'Umu aya Biafra—what have they been up to now?' she wondered. She sat up in the dark and would not wake her husband in the big house until she was quite sure what the trouble was. The noise grew louder and nearer. So she came out of the hut, and the words 'Death, abomination, death, Umu aya Biafra' reached her. This was serious.

She wrapped her night waist-cloth around her and ran, shouting: 'Obi Agiliga, wake up, they say that Umu aya Biafra have killed somebody, wake up.' As she shouted and ran across the compound she went straight to the spare hut which the boys of the compound shared. She breathed a sigh of relief when she saw Okei, spread out in sleep next to his cousin Onuoha. 'So whatever it is, we have nothing to do with it.'

'What is it now, what are you shouting for?' Obi Agiliga shouted at his first wife.

'Just listen, listen to the whole Igbuno. They are saying that Umu aya Biafra have killed and burgled somebody— I don't know who.'

'Oh my God, oh my God. These young boys. What of our son?' asked the Obi, now surrounded by most of the males in his compound.

'He is there, still sleeping.'

'Then he has nothing to do with it. Wake him up. I must find out from him first.'

Okei was still drowsy with sleep when he was led into Obi Agiliga's courtyard. 'Now, I want to know everything. Don't leave anything behind. You know what our people say, that the day of blood relatives, friends would go? This night is the night of blood relatives. If we are going into a knife-fight to defend this compound, we must know the truth first. Who have you sent to go and kill somebody, Okei?'

Okei wanted to be sarcastic as usual, but he sensed the seriousness and urgency of the occasion. He shook his head violently, anger giving him strength. 'I don't know anything about it. I did not send anybody to burgle or steal or kill . . . .'

'But they say that you are the leader. You did not feel us important enough to hear it from your own lips, but I know. So if you are the leader and an abomination has been committed in the name of your age-group, you should be the first to know. I believe you did not do it'—here Agiliga smiled a little—'and I believe you have nothing to do with it. No son of Agiliga would tell a lie to his own people.'

'I am sorry, Father, I did not tell you about my nomination. I did not know that such a thing would interest you. I thought you would laugh at me.'

'A leader is a leader, son, and this harvest-time is your coming-of-age time, and it is an important age in any man's life. But let all that be. Who could have done this, and for what reason?' Okei's mind went to giggling Uche, who had to muddle the Akpei stream just to annoy people —but killing a person? No, he did not think Uche could do such a thing. He did not have such a courage. Again Okei shrugged his shoulders and shook his head. 'I don't know, really I don't know.'

'You had a gathering a few nights ago. You did not discuss anything like that?' Agiliga persisted.

'Discuss a thing like what?' Nne Ojo asked. 'I was there in my hut, and I could hear all that they said. How I laughed about it all. They were just boys, groping their way to life. They discussed many things—wrestling, announcing this and that—but not killing or stealing. I can swear for my little husband Okei. But who would do a thing like this, to discredit a group of innocent boys, for God's sake?'

'All right, woman. Say no more until we know the full story. We know where we stand now.'

So saying, he changed from his sleeping-loincloth and put on a pair of shorts which he covered with an outer otuogwu cloth. He frightened his family when he took out two curved knives and a cutlass and slung them around his waist. Nne Ojo started to cry when she saw them.

'But Okei did not do anything, Agiliga!'

'People do not know that now. They may know later, but meanwhile some stupid people may take it upon themselves to revenge on the leader of the age-group. You see, son, why it's no easy thing being a leader. I must go and find out.'

'I am going with you,' Okei said, standing out.

'That is good, son, but you can't and you won't. This time, you will obey me. I am your father's brother, born of the same parents. I am your father alive. You must do what I say. Nne Ojo, take the boy and hide him in your hut. No respectable man would search the wife of an Obi, to say nothing of the hut of his senior wife. You and the others just keep awake, and if anybody asks for me and Okei say we have gone to find out what is happening in Igbuno.'

'Oh, father, suppose they attack you in anger, when you have nothing to do with it? I will go with you to prove our innocence,' Okei begged, near tears.

'No son of Agiliga cries in the presence of the women in his compound. If you must do that, go and do it in private.'

With that he left his family. And Nne Ojo's grip on Okei's wrist tightened as she led him into her hut.

Obi Agiliga had scarcely left when two angry young men burst into his compound, demanding to have a word with Okei. But Nne Ojo had hidden him in the darkest part of her hut, where he could hear nothing from the outside. She sat in her front room, peeping at the two men. 'Only two people? Well, we can cope with those.' She did not come out, but allowed the hired labourers who were still staying in the compound to deal with them. She could hear every word that was being uttered, and could see them all too clearly.

'They have gone to the centre of Igbuno to see why everybody was shouting "Murder, murder",' said the labourers in their imperfect Igbo.

'They? Who are they?' asked one of the young men.

'Oh, the two people you are looking for. Obi Agiliga and his nephew Okei.'

'Are all the members of this family dead, then? How come we can only have a word with hired labourers who can scarcely understand us?' one of the men asked in a loud voice of insolence.

Obi Agiliga's youngest wife was pregnant. She knew that they would not dare do any harm to her, and she could not stand there in the shadow and hear her compound insulted. Nne Ojo, she knew, was watching her and keeping an eye on Okei. So she came out from the corner of the compound, rubbing her eyes as if she had been woken from sleep. 'What do we owe that you should come and visit us this time of night? Anyway, welcome. Our father has gone out, so we can't give you kola nut and palm-wine.'

'Are you the only compound in Igbuno that has not heard all that has been going on for the past hours?'

'What has been going on?' the young wife demanded, stressing her innocence by opening her eyes wide.

'Have you not heard that Obi Uju has almost killed his beloved daughter Kwutelu, all because of a son of this compound?'

'Almost killed her? She is alive, then?'

'Do you want her dead? My brother in Ilorin has paid for her bride-price, and now she has only one ear. Her father has sliced the other one off.'

'Oh dear, oh dear. And what has our Okei got to do with it?'

'What has he got to do with it? He threatened Kwutelu this morning by the stream that he would burgle her father's compound. So when she came in late her father thought it was your Okei, and cut her ear by mistake.'

'I am sorry you are going to marry a young bride with only one ear . . .' the young wife began, but she could not help laughing, and all the others who had been listening to the conversation started with a ripple of laughter and then laughed out loud.

Nne Ojo knew that it was time for her to take over. Thank goodness the girl is alive, she thought.

She welcomed the two angry men again and expressed her sorrow. It was a very nasty accident, and they should take it so. The Europeans could fix a new ear for their wife. They could use a piece of brown rubber; it would look like a brand new ear. 'It's no use crying for revenge. Okei could have threatened to burgle Obi Uju's compound but he has not done it. And don't forget that Kwutelu is also of the same age-group. So you two come here to fight a small boy of sixteen? I am sure you are older than him by at least ten years. I am sorry for what has happened, though. But you all know how our people settle such things, by wrestling openly for the truth.'

'Who will wrestle with that ninny? I'll break his bones in pieces.'

'You see, we are saying the same thing. Okei is just a baby, and you two come here to revenge your wife-to-be's ear with knives . . . .'

'We haven't got any knives on us. We are not murderers.'

'Then please go back to your compound and sleep off your anger. I am sorry about your wife's ear.'

The two young men left shamefacedly. And Nne Ojo tried very hard to hush the laughter that would have overtaken all the members of Obi Agiliga's compound. She went back to her hut and said to Okei: 'Go back to sleep. All is well.'

When Obi Agiliga returned to his compound some time later, he and his senior wife stayed in the middle of their compound and went through the whole episode. They both agreed that Obi Uju had been a bit high-handed. 'Suppose he had killed his daughter, all because she had an argument with Okei, and an argument which she started,' Obi Agiliga wondered.

The Obi asked Nne Ojo whether she had told Okei anything. She said she had not, because she hid him in the darkest part of her hut. 'But,' she added, 'the boy is sleeping now. I think he is beginning to trust us at last. He knew that you would take care of everything.'

'Yes, let him sleep. I can see the faces of those mischievous boys in the morning. They say that Kwutelu has been a pain in the neck to them. Most of them did not like her very much. She is very cheeky.'

'Oh, Obi Agiliga, the poor girl does not deserve to lose an ear just because she was cheeky,' Nne Ojo said.

She made her way back to her hut, and slept soundly till morning.

8

Okei woke up and for a time wondered where he was. Then the happenings of the night came flooding through his mind. He wondered at the whole set-up and would have liked to know exactly what had taken place. No one would tell him. In any case, it was too early for people to get up from their sleeping-places. He had now become used to getting up early, so he crept out of Nne Ojo's hut and jogged down to the stream's incline, hoping to have covered several rounds of his daily running exercises before Nduka arrived. Once or twice an eel of fear wriggled in his stomach, but he calmed himself by remembering what Nne Ojo had said to him before his going to sleep. Had she not said, 'Go back to sleep, all is well' to him? He knew that Nne Ojo, being the senior wife, would never make a statement like that for fun. All must be well.

As he ran up and down the incline breathing heavily, feeling the strength building up in his young, thin but strong legs, a kind of confidence was gradually building inside him as well. In a wrestling match a contender was on the lose if he allowed his opponent to floor him. But if one had a pair of very strong legs that could stand the pushing and thumping and still be on one's feet, then that one was bound to win. He sometimes wondered who his opponent was going to be.

During his runs he disturbed many little animals who had been sleeping in peace before his arrival on the scene. Here he heard one angry bird singing croakily out of tune, as if in protest to his being there. There he saw a bush rabbit scurrying away into safety, no doubt wondering why such a person as Okei should take it upon himself to disturb them so. All the animals could not help hearing him, because the fallen, yellowing, dry leaves made loud crackling noises on his approach, like corn popping in an open fire. Never mind, little animals. The fight will be towards the end of the harvest, and then you will not see me again here to come and disturb your peace.

Then he stopped short. He heard a laughter that sounded more like that of a bush monkey than that of any human he had known. 'Surely this part of the forest is too close to human habitation for monkeys to come this close,' Okei thought as he looked around him, wondering whether he had imagined it. Then he heard the laughter again, this time closer to him, and with this second bout of uncontrollable, unnecessary laughter Uche, his friend and age-mate, emerged from that part of the forest that jutted itself into the pathway. He had been crouching there, watching him no doubt.

'I was not expecting to see you here this morning. Since when have you decided to come and exercise with me?' said Okei angrily.

'I know you were expecting Nduka, but I come early because I wish to congratulate you for what happened last night.'

'What happened?'

'Have they not told you? They thought we cut Kwutelu's ear. It is so funny.' Uche started to laugh again.

Okei was not amused, but was willing to wait for Uche to control himself before asking him for the full story. Uche was only too happy to comply. He told the story, dancing his demonstrations, making this funny sound and that silly one, just as if he had been there when Obi Uju was sharpening the knife with which he had accidentally sliced his daughter's ear. Okei had to laugh loud as Uche mimicked Obi Uju's cries of agony when he realized his mistake.

'. . . And of course early this morning I decided to go and see and show my sympathy to Kwutelu. But when I saw her, I could not laugh. Eh, you know something, that girl is really sick now. I saw her ear in a calabash bowl. They had to tie her hair with bandages and a scarf. They are taking her to the big hospital in Benin. Her father is still crying and cursing us all, especially you. I told them how sorry we are, and do you know, Kwutelu could not talk . . . .'

'Who could not talk?' Nduka asked as he sprang on them from the part of the forest that jutted into the pathway.

'Kwutelu!' Okei replied in astonishment. 'Have you ever heard of a thing like that before? That Kwutelu could not talk?'

'I can't believe it. I think her father did a nasty job. I think he ought to have cut her tongue or even her lips, instead of her innocent ear. Her future husband would not thank him for the loss of her ear, but he would thank him for the loss of her abusive tongue.'

'Oh, but we are awful,' Okei said, becoming thoughtful as his mood changed. 'We should really be sorry for the poor soul, not making fun of her like this.'

'But that sharpened knife was meant for you, Okei,' Uche pointed out.

'You did not believe for a moment that I was going there to steal anything? What I said was that if I had known those who did the burgling I would gladly tell them to come and burgle her father's compound. But of course she changed the story, to sensationalize it for her father. And now he has overreacted . . . . Pity. Come, let's go on with our wrestling practice.'

'You don't need to do that too seriously any more. This incident has shown that God is on our side,' Uche said, wanting to back out from the rigorous exercise.

'Have you not heard that heavens help those who help themselves? God will not come down and wrestle with the Akpei boys for us. We will have to do it. He may help us if he wished, but the Akpei boys will be praying to him too,' Okei said.

'That sounds like what one of my teachers used to say,' Nduka replied. 'He claimed to have known somebody who had been a prisoner on both sides in the last war. He said that the person said that each side prayed to God to be on their side.'

'The man who had known another who had been in the great war said that somebody said—Gosh, you make me dizzy,' laughed Uche. 'That may be so, but I am not going to kill myself running and wrestling. I am going to the market-place to watch Kwutelu go to the big hospital in Benin. The mammy lorry will be there soon. And in particular I want to watch a crying Obi and a dumb Kwutelu. I wouldn't miss that scene for all the wrestling matches in the world.'

He left his two friends and faced the path towards home. Then he added for a good measure: 'I will tell you all about it when I see you later in the day.'

'Yes, and all garnished and spiced to your taste,' Nduka said, and Okei laughed.

Uche went back into the village, and Okei asked Nduka if he had told the others to practise wrestling as he had advised them to do. Nduka had already done so and this pleased Okei. With that they went into the hard work of catching each other's legs and thumbing one another's arms and stomach to toughen all their young muscles.

*

At that moment, Obi Uwechue paid an early visit to Obi Agiliga on the farm. He had heard rumours of knifing, he said, and he wanted to know whether it was true that Umu aya Biafra had started it all.

'How news flies,' marvelled Obi Agiliga.

He soon told his friend from Akpei how it all happened, and they were both sorry, because they knew that indirectly they had encouraged the girls to goad the boys into anger. They agreed that the accident could have been worse. 'Suppose Obi Uju had killed his daughter outright?' Obi Uwechu pondered aloud.

After a pause, he went on: 'There is one good thing that is arising from all this—we do not have boys molesting anyone in the footpath any more. They are all busy practising their wrestling and getting angry at the insults the other party is heaping on them.'

'Have you noticed that in Akpei too? But for the last night's incident, the aya Biafra boys in Igbuno had been busy holding meetings and getting themselves toughened.'

'Well, that is the whole point of the whole exercise, isn't it?' asked Obi Uwechue.

'You are right, my friend, after this incident they will learn to think a little like adults. Even my nephew is beginning to look at me as if I am somebody at last. Before, I was just an old man to be shouted at.'

The two elders chuckled knowingly at their cleverness. They had successfully created problems for the 'know-all' youngsters.

9

It was another Eke market. There was much excitement in the air, and the girls of Igbuno were determined to make the best of the few Eke markets left. They would sell their heavy load of plantain as expensively as they possibly could; they would need the money to buy the latest colourful outfits. The relation between them and the boys was still uncertain, but a few boys had already made it up with some of their girl-friends. Even Kwutelu had started to exchange polite praise-greetings.

'Lord, your neck will sink into your chest with that big bunch of bananas,' Josephine's mother observed. 'It is too heavy. Why don't you sell them here? You will make some profit with such a big bunch.'

'But I will make even more profit in Akpei. All my friends are going there this Eke market with as big a bunch as they can carry. I am not the only one.'

'These modern girls and their love for money,' Josephine's mother said, shaking her head.

Josephine balanced the bunch on the piece of old cloth she had coiled, and placed it all on her head. Yes, it was heavy, but the picture of the latest abada cloth she was going to wear on the day of the wrestling match was already imprinted in her mind. She had to work hard and save the money.

At the main crossing she saw some of her friends waiting for her. They all carried much heavier bunches than usual.

'I hope the Akpei people will buy all your plantain,' said an old woman cynically, looking at them with contempt.

'I don't know why some people won't mind their business,' said Josephine in a low voice.

'Well, if they all do mind their business, they won't be the people of Igbuno,' Kwutelu said. She then looked around her enviously and continued: 'My bunch is the size of a small girl's. I don't know why that old woman did not make any remark about that.'

'Don't talk like that, Kwutelu. When you were well we all know that you used to carry the biggest bunches of plantain of any of us. You must not carry anything big now, because it gives you headache,' said Josephine consolingly.

Kwutelu sighed and was silent. This was the new attitude people noticed about her since the accident. Some thought that maybe she stopped being abusive because she was frightened in case people would call her 'rubber ear'. Because, as Nne Ojo had foretold on the night of the accident, an artificial ear had been glued to her head.

The spirit of the girls soon became light as they jogged their way to Akpei. They chattered about empty nothings as they climbed the steep hill that led to Akpei.

They arrived there very early as usual, hoping that by so doing they would sell their wares and leave for home early. After waiting for a while for the market to get full, they noticed that nobody from Akpei had come to ask them for their plantain. 'Maybe they have stopped eating plantain,' Josephine said with a nervous giggle.

'It's still early yet,' Kwutelu said confidently.

47

The market became full and people started going home, yet all the Igbuno girls stood there staring at their unsold plantain.

'Do you think they are doing this on purpose?' a little girl of fourteen asked Kwutelu.

'But I don't know either. Maybe they too are going off food in order to save for their yam festival and the wrestling match,' Kwutelu replied.

'It will be funny and humiliating if we have to go back home still carrying our bunches of plantain,' Josephine remarked.

Kwutelu and the others were thinking of the same thing. They would be disappointed, to say nothing of the shame of it. Still, they all agreed to stay a little longer.

'I am so hungry,' cried one girl in despair.

'You are not the only one,' Josephine replied to her.

Normally by this time they would have almost finished selling and would have some food for themselves. But this afternoon they still had their plantain untouched by any customer, so there was no money to buy food.

Then came an old woman. She was in dark-patterned abada cloth and was walking with a stick, peering this way and that way critically as some old people do. She stopped in front of the girls and, having appraised them, advised them to give their plantain away to poor old people like herself. That way the bunches of plantain would be useful. 'If you stand here all day and night, nobody will buy your plantain.'

'But why, why?' Kwutelu cried.

'You ask me why?' she asked as she shook her stick in the air. 'I shall tell you. Our Umu aya Biafra are planning a friendly wrestling match with your boys, and what do you think your boys are doing by turning the whole thing upside down?'

'Turning it upside down? What is she talking about?' the girls asked one another.

But the woman did not answer. Her mind went on to other things. 'If you carry a bunch of your plantain to my hut, I will always bless you. If you take all your wares home, they will go rotten on you. If you think you are going to sell them here in Akpei, you will wait for ever.' She went down the market square, still peering this way and that.

'What are we going to do?' cried Josephine. 'If I have to carry that bunch back all the way to Igbuno I will never recover from the shame. Do you think we should ask them why they are boycotting our part of the market, Kwutelu?'

'And be insulted into the bargain? No, Josephine the daughter of Nwogbu, we won't stoop that low. We can dump some of the plantain in the bush on our way home if they are too heavy, but if not we must take them back to Igbuno with us. Can't you see what is happening, the way those people are looking at us slyly and laughing? All this was not accident. I know that we are hungry and tired, but we must go. And as far as I am concerned, I will always support my own people. I will always sell my plantain in our own Eke market, not come to a place like this and be insulted. You remove that woebegone look from your face, it is not the end of the world.' Kwutelu finished addressing the latter part of her speech to the youngest girl, Adaobi, who had previously complained of hunger.

They packed their plantain again and helped each other into putting them on their heads, then went down the road leading to Igbuno, forcing themselves to make light jokes as if this type of thing happened to them every market day. They could hear people, one or two knots of gossip loungers, laughing out loudly. But the girls went on with determined steps.

When they knew that they were far from Akpei, they did away with their mask of pretence.

'Goodbye to my dream abada material,' Josephine moaned.

'And welcome to our village pride. From now on we will

have to boost the ego of our boys, not deflect it. The people of Akpei have turned a harmless joke into something serious,' Kwutelu was quiet for a while, realizing that all these rumours had almost cost her her life. So it must be serious.

Halfway between Akpei and Igbuno some of the girls threw away their plantain because they knew that they had a lot at home and it could not keep very long. They were all tired and could scarcely carry themselves, to say nothing of taking home heavy bundles of plantain which seemed to have become doubly weighty.

'It does not matter very much if we appear at the wrestling-square in our old abada cloth,' said Kwutelu. 'After all, the way the Akpei people are going about it, I don't think it is going to be all that friendly.'

'Yes, that will be a good idea. Let us make it an old abada cloth day. Those silly Akpei girls will come in their very best, then we can pick up quarrel with them and mess their new outfits. Yes, that will teach them,' said Josephine mischievously.

They all laughed, despite their failure to sell their plantain.

They were still laughing when they came to the hill bordering the Igbuno stream. They were met by a larger group of people, because many of their parents were anxious about them. It was a moonless night and very dark. But the friends and relatives met them with lamps and hand-torches.

The girls poured out their story and the young men became really incensed, determined to win the match.

But when the male elders heard it all later in the night, they all smiled with a conspiratorial wink.

10

The next gathering of the Umu aya Biafra was held on a moonless night. The night was dark and forbidding. All the familiar trees and everyday shapes acquired greater solidity. Some trees even seemed to be moving when the night breeze fanned the landscape. The age-group carried hurricane lamps, and some modern and well-to-do boys brought powerful hand-torches.

This time they decided not to meet in the open, after their experience of the last meeting. They were moody almost to the last person. The insults, jibes, and abuses of the young men and women of Akpei had aroused the anger of the mildest member. Even Uche, who was always thought to be easy-going, had taken it almost as a personal insult that the Igbuno girls were shunned in Akpei market. So they met in an old abandoned hut at the corner of Akpuenu. This hut was large and used for occasional dance-practices. The boys did not know who owned it, but they knew that they would not be chased away.

The matter of Kwutelu's ear was mentioned briefly.

Some still found it funny, but many were beginning to feel sorry for Kwutelu, especially as she had now changed for the better.

Everybody was then allowed to display the tricks of wrestling they had mastered since their last gathering. They had fun with this, because there were those who were born to be non-wrestlers. Uche, for example, was always looking for a nice, soft place to fall instead of defending himself. 'Oh, Uche, you wrestle like a pregnant woman,' Okei shouted at the top of the laughter.

There was a big hush when Okei chose Nduka as a partner. The others were intrigued by the quickness of the two wrestlers, their lightness of touch, and the clever way with which they were polite to each other. It was a kind of wrestling, but a wrestling with an art. It was beautiful to watch. But the farmer boys among them started to grumble. The grumble became loud, and Okei had to stop the wrestling.

'And what is your problem, farmer's boy from Ogbeukwu?' he asked.

The so-addressed disregarded the insolent tone and answered sharply. 'This is like a white man's wrestling, you two dancing about each other as if you are playing hide and seek. It is beautiful to watch, it is amusing. But it will not do for those Akpei people. Remember that I had to take message of the wrestle to them. I saw the spirit with which my news was received. They were determined. This type of dancing will win nothing for us.'

'So how do you want us to wrestle?' asked Okei, panting with anger and breathless.

'The way real wrestlers wrestle.'

Others applauded the statement from the farmer's boy. 'After all, we elected you to be our leader. You should do your best to retain the post.'

'I am not afraid of the leadership being taken away from me . . . .' Okei began.

'Ahem, ahem,' Uche butted in. 'I like the dance, as you said, but where can we learn to improve it? Okei is very fast and strong, but if we can help him to be better it will be much more helpful than arguing about it.' Then he started to laugh.

'You have made a good contribution,' said the farmer's boy, 'but I don't know why you are laughing. I saw the Akpei boys consulting with their elders even whilst I was still there. Okei can consult his uncle. They say that he was a good heavy wrestler in his time. Why can't we use his knowledge? I am sure he will be willing to teach us.'

'No! No! This is our war, this is our problem. We don't want the elders to nose into our business. So keep him out of it. I won't like to consult with him for anything,' Okei yelled, his voice echoing round the hushed gathering as if he were the only person there.

'But the Akpei young people are being helped by their elders,' Nduka put in pointedly. 'Why can't we use their knowledge too?'

'Because we are doing our thing our own way. We don't want their ways. They are old-fashioned, and as for my uncle . . . well, he is not bad for an uncle, but I don't like consulting him for anything.'

'Then we are fighting a losing battle,' the farmer's boy said, 'because the young people of Akpei are bound to come out on top. And listen, Okei, are you going to do without the wrestling dance too? You know you will have to dance round the circle in a certain way. None of us here knows the wordings of the song, to say nothing of the way to dance it. Your uncle is a master at it. Are you going to do without that too?'

Okei looked at him in the dim light for a long time. Had they made a mistake in allowing those who had never sat behind desks at school to come and join them? Could they not do without the dance? A wrestling match without its dance was half a show, he knew. He must give in.

'. . . We need our elders,' the farmer's boy continued. 'After all, they are our fathers, and they cannot direct us wrong. This is going to be a friendly match, and I hope it remains so. But suppose it should go out of hand?'

'All right, you have made your point. I'll see what help he can give us, to polish up our way of wrestling. I suppose one has to look up to one's elders.'

'A village that has no elders has no future. I hope we will always have elders,' Nduka said prayerfully.

11

It was easy for Okei's age-mates to suggest that he should seek advice from his uncle, Obi Agiliga. He saw the point of his not making the mistakes which the elders had made before him. But until now it had never occurred to him that he and his age-mates could make mistakes at all. 'Blast those Akpei boys! Why should they take it upon themselves to seek advice from their elders?' How was he going to start telling his troubles to his uncle? A man he had looked upon with tolerance, that type of tolerance that had to exist because there was no way out for him, because he had no other place to live. He feared that his uncle would feel proud and would hint, 'I have always thought you would come to me to ask for advice.'

'It is that humiliating part that I resent so much,' he confessed to Nduka the second day. 'I would have liked us to do without the likes of my uncle completely.'

'Well, we can't, and we won't. We need the likes of him. What is wrong with his feeling proud about our seeking his advice? You never know, in a few years time it will be your turn to advise his young sons. You will be the elder in your family then. Would it be wrong of you to feel proud then? I don't know what you are worrying about.'

'I resented my parents' death and maybe his staying alive. Maybe if he had been my father and not my uncle, I would have been able to go to him naturally.'

'Well, he cannot help staying alive, can he? It's not his fault your parents were killed. It was a war, and you and I know that in such wars, the innocent suffer. Don't lose the match for us because of your pride and stubbornness. I shall come with you, if you so desire.'

'Thank you very much. I think that this is a family matter. I shall deal with it alone. Come on, let us run down the slope one more time.'

Obi Agiliga was surprised to see Okei sitting in his courtyard in the evening. He was behaving in the normal traditional way, of sitting around in the evening after the day's work had been done and listening to the conversations of the adults and learning lessons from them. Agiliga glanced at him uneasily once or twice, and wondered what had come upon him. But he controlled himself from asking him any questions.

Okei helped in serving the adults the ever-present kola nuts and palm-wine, betraying no emotion but being extremely polite. One or two of Agiliga's friends who knew Okei's reputation arched their brows in a question, and Obi Agiliga simply shrugged his shoulders. He did not know the reason for this change of heart.

Okei started clearing and tidying up when the visitors had left. Agiliga watched him as he smoked his last pipe before retiring for the night. Then he asked: 'What is it, Okei? What is worrying you?'

Okei looked up at his uncle and smiled. 'It is the wrestling match,' he replied promptly.

'You want to learn the songs and the style we used. Our style.'

Okei would have liked to find out how his uncle knew exactly what he wanted, but he was so taken in by its suddenness that he nodded enthusiastically.

Then his uncle—who was also a tall man, but whose tallness was less pronounced because of his thickened body —got out from his sitting-place and took two simple but cunning steps towards Okei, and by the time he realized what he was doing Okei found himself lying on the floor.

He got up and glared at his uncle. Obi Agiliga roared with laughter and said, 'That is not a very fair way to treat your wrestling opponent. But if everything fails, it is a useful art to master. I will teach you that first.'

Obi Agiliga did not stop with teaching him how to take his opponent unawares, especially if the person became violent; he taught him how to give his audience pleasure by luring his opponent round and round and then suddenly confronting him. 'Most opponents are not prepared for this sudden halt, and you have to use their unpreparedness to floor them. You know that if an opponent's back reaches the ground, then you have won.'

'I know that, uncle,' Okei said with his mouth full of laughter at this Obi who in his enthusiasm had been transformed into an agile young man. He worked up his body into lumps and hooks, displaying many methods of trapping an opponent. It looked for a while as if the Obi was simply displaying his art only for himself. He became completely unaware of Okei's presence. Okei's respect for his uncle really soared high.

When it came to the words of the wrestling song, Obi Agiliga became supple and almost soft as a woman. he would jump into the air, and just as you thought he was going to land flatly on his back, you would see him touching the ground as lightly as a fallen dry leaf. Then like a cat he would tread softly on the balls of his feet, singing and moving to the rhythm of his own music.

He was thus preoccupied when his senior wife Nne Ojo

came in. Okei made a sign for her to be quiet, and the two of them watched Obi Agiliga perform. It was only when he had danced to his heart's content that he said, 'Now I have to teach you all that.'

Nne Ojo laughed with tears in her eyes. 'I used to see you in the wrestling circle performing like that. To think that you were that young once.'

'Yes, that was a long time ago,' the Obi said with some confusion. 'I have to teach it all to this young man here. It is his turn now. My turn has come and gone.'

'It was a lovely time, when we were always young,' Nne Ojo said, and walked across the courtyard, making for the door leading into one of the rooms.

'Don't go, my senior wife. I was the leader of the wrestling group of my age, but not the leader of my age-group. But Okei here is the leader of his age-group and is required to defend their reputation. So it will be a big occasion for this family. Could you let him borrow one of your red Akwete cloths to use as a kind of cloak? I want him to come out in style to beat those crude Akpei boys. It is not always that a wrestling leader is also elected as the leader of his age-group. You will get the whole compound ready as well.'

'We have done all the preparation in secret, hoping that one day our Okei will ask for your help. Now he has done it, we will all be behind him.'

'Yes, that is right. The Akpei people and the whole of Igbuno will not forget the year in which Okei the son of Agiliga came of age,' Obi Agiliga said proudly.

Nne Ojo soon left them and the two men, one middle-aged, the other a youth, practised the art and songs of wrestling till late at night.

12

The people of Igbuno, in their fever of excitement, started to count the days by saying that the day of the great wrestling match had only two market days to go. Then they started to count the days. It would be in four days' time, then three, then two, eventually the day after tomorrow.

Okei and his friend Nduka had become village heroes. As they practised in the early morning they now had a large group of young enthusiasts who came to watch them. It was during the school holidays, and those boys who went to the farms were all free because the yams had been harvested. They cheered as the two boys punched each other mercilessly. They applauded as they danced in their art. They ran up and down the incline with them until they were out of breath. It was a time of great hope.

All the boys of that age went to a special barber, who had to cut their hair in a certain style called the Appian Way. So they were easily recognizable. The old, the young men, and the women prayed for them to win the wrestling match.

'Our own age-group has got an original touch,' boasted Uche as he trotted and puffed like a dog behind Okei and Nduka.

'What master touch?' Okei asked.

'All age-groups until now usually come out with some lousy dances. But we are wrestling our way into manhood.'

'Maybe because we saw the gunning down and killing of many people in our babyhood.'

'But that is true, though,' Okei put in to enlighten his friend Nduka. 'I keep wondering why it never occurred to us to dance our way out.'

'It never occurred to us,' said Nduka.

'But why since that would have been the normal thing?'

'I don't know. Don't ask me,' Uche replied with a sickening giggle.

At home in Agiliga's compound, Okei was being treated to a place of honour. He was always being invited to eat with the Obi. He was no longer ordered to go and eat with the women, so Nne Ojo could not complain about his nasty eating manner. Once he started to eat with the elders, he began to behave himself.

Amidst the excitement and expectation, Okei asked Obi Agiliga one evening: 'Suppose, father, I lose the contest?'

'In the first place, you will not lose. In the second place, even if you lost, it won't be a complete loss because you would have added a new art to the game of wrestling, and you would have taken part and done your best. Don't you think it is better to think on those lines, Okei the son of Agiliga?'

'You are right, father.'

They had just finished their evening meal, the day before the official yam festival day, when they were suddenly forced to listen to a group of dancers coming towards the Agiliga's compound. As they drew nearer, the words of their songs became more distinct.

They were singing:

'Akpei people bumkum,
The world bumkum, we don't care.
Why should we care?
When we have heroes like Okei . . . .
Heroes like Okei the son of Agiliga
In our midst.'

They came to the front gate of the compound and made a
circle. The dancers were the very girls who only a few
months ago had been against the boys of Umu aya Biafra.

Kwutelu and another girl led the singing in turns. The
rest of the group answered, shaking their beaded gourds in
the air. They were so organized that the circle was never
crowded. There were never more than two girls in the circle
at the same time. Their male guide had a mock whip in his
hands, ready to chase any unwanted dancer who was not
invited to join in. So great was the happiness and excitement that everybody wished to display their own special
dance. They kept on and on calling Okei to come out and
dance for them. He would not. And people thought he was
shy.

'I will dance for him,' said the senior wife of the family,
Nne Ojo. Her dance was a little comical, and it was clear
that she was putting it on on purpose. She knew she could
not crouch and jump as quickly and as gracefully as the
young girls, so she overdid her stiff back. She placed one
hand on her hip, and walked round the circle in imitation
of the girls. She made faces at them, until the drummers
and singers all collapsed in laughter.

'You must go and make a few dancing steps, Okei, at
least to show your appreciation for all the girls' efforts,'
Obi Agiliga advised.

'I can't believe Kwutelu is singing my praises. She used
to laugh at me.'

'Everyone loves a winner,' his uncle said wisely.

Okei eventually sprinted into the circle, dancing lightly

as if he were a bird in flight. When he crouched slightly to the music, he looked like a bird pecking some food with its beak and then taking flight. He was so light. He was so agile, and they loved him.

The dancers were entertained, and they sang their way to other compounds. Everybody knew that the yam festival had started.

13

The wrestling match day did arrive at last. The dawn was misty, but it was clear even from that early morning mist that it was going to be a sunny and dry day. No one expected it to rain at this time of year, but one could never tell for sure, especially as it was possible for some people who were not well disposed to the wrestling to intone to the skies and make it rain.

Okei was awakened by the drums of Igbuno. The special drummers knew how to make their drums talk and convey messages. This used to be a common thing a very, very long time ago. But now, these drums were used only on important occasions like this.

The doubt still lingered in Okei's mind. He had never been beaten in wrestling before, in Igbuno. But he did not know the style the opponents from Akpei would use. He did not let anybody know of his fear though, but he was determined to take his uncle's advice and do his best. And if he should lose, to accept it gallantly.

He was not left on his sleeping-mat long. Excited voices rang round the compound as young mothers called their children for the stream and their morning bath. The smell of roasted yams wafted all over the compound and the whole village. Smoke from wood fires rose from here and there and everywhere. On yam festival wrestling match days, even the poorest widow could afford to dip a whole yam into the open fire. When roasted, they were dipped in palm-oil and slightly salted and peppered. The crust of that roasted yam was a great treat for both children and adults. Okei knew that at least on this his great day, the crust of the yams would be left for him. At the thought of this, it looked to him as if the aroma of the food was strengthened especially for his nose. He got up and walked into the open compound.

'Oh, my strong little husband will come to my hut and eat my roasted yam?' Obi Agiliga's youngest wife asked hopefully.

Unfortunately for her, Nne Ojo was not too far away. She gave the young woman such a look that sent her scurrying like a squirrel into her own hut. 'You must be careful of what you eat and where you eat today, Okei,' she said.

Okei had to suppress the urge to show his eagerness. He was dying to have a taste, but he said manfully: 'I must go to the stream to have a bath first.'

'Well, don't stay too long and don't practise any more,' Obi Agiliga shouted from the verandah of his house. He had heard all that Nne Ojo and his youngest wife had been saying. 'When you return, your yam, specially prepared for you, will be here, hot and waiting.'

At the stream many people wished Okei luck from afar. He acknowledged them all with a nod. Meeting Nduka at the mens' area relaxed him a little.

'Did you see Kwutelu and the others last night?' Nduka asked.

'Yes, they came to our compound, and she was singing my praises,' Okei said with a laugh.

64

'Did you not notice that all the girls were wearing their headscarves like a band, to cover their ears and display their hairdos?'

'I thought that was their latest fashion or something,' Okei said naïvely.

'Well, it could become fashionable. But Kwutelu started it, to cover her damaged ear, and she willed the style so strongly on the other girls that it was accepted as part of their dancing outfit.'

Both boys laughed conspiratorially.

'Poor Kwutelu,' Okei said in sympathy.

'We have to hurry home, and good luck to you. The Akpei people are taking this very seriously, I heard,' Nduka said.

'As far as we are concerned, it is a friendly match between the same age-groups. The adults can come and watch, but they must not interfere. We will choose our own judges and referees from both sides. They will be of the same age as all of us. Nothing to do with the adults and nothing at all that serious.'

'Well, you'll have to warn the Igbuno girls. They see this wrestling match as a way of revenging the bad treatment they received over their plantain issue.'

'That was their fault,' said Okei. 'We have an Eke market here in Igbuno. Why go all that way just to sell them? Yes, I know they make a few pennies extra. But if for any reason they have to go by a car or a bus of some kind, that money would be eroded.'

'Anyway, few cars run that road. And they have stopped going to Akpei now. Yet they still want to use this match to get even with them.'

Okei shrugged his shoulders. The two boys soon parted, each to his own compound to go and get ready for the wrestling.

By the afternoon there were drums being beaten in every big compound in Igbuno. People put on their best clothes,

65

and went round to relatives' houses to eat yams and exchange gifts of yams. Everything and everybody was yammy. There would still be many dances for the rest of the season, but on wrestling match day the excitement was at its highest.

'Ah, I can hear a different kind of drum from ours,' Obi Agiliga remarked. 'And I think it is the Akpei people. They must be nearing our hill.' He watched Nne Ojo, his senior wife, put the last touches on the Akwete cloak Okei was going to wear.

Okei, who had been lying on the mud couch in the courtyard, sat and listened carefully. Yes, he could hear a faint rhythm, different from the other, nearer ones. It was so faint that he had to strain his ears to hear it. Then he smiled at his uncle and said: 'You have been expecting that sound, have you not?'

Obi Agiliga nodded, puffing confidently at his pipe. 'Are you boys not having any elders there to see to the smooth running of things?'

'No, father, we are boys of a new breed. We want to do most of the whole things by ourselves. But since the Akpei boys consulted their elders to give them some tips, I had to come to you to teach me the tricky bits of wrestling and the dance to it. But you have helped us this far, I think we can now go on by ourselves. You all are invited to come and watch, though.'

Obi Agiliga smiled into the smoke from his pipe. 'You don't invite people to watch anything in Igbuno. We just go. And as far back as I can remember, the yam festival was always climaxed by boys on the verge of manhood entertaining everybody with a dance of some sort. But in your case, you want to celebrate yours with a fight.'

'Not a fight, father. A sport.'

'Well that may be so. But some people are not so good at losing. You must remember that. In any case, the whole village will be there.'

66

The other people in the compound gave a shout of delight and cried, 'We will show them, we will show them.'

'They have heard the Akpei drums too. They are talking drums, and are saying that their wrestlers are the greatest and fastest wrestlers in the whole of Nigeria,' explained Obi Agiliga.

'Is that what they are saying? I must get ready. We must go and meet them in style.'

The men in the compound helped Okei to dress up. He only wore a plain pair of shorts and a pair of colourful plimsolls to match. But on top of this, he had several charms slung round his neck. One of them was made with crocodile teeth, to prevent him from becoming breathless. Another was from nut kernels, to harden him like nuts which are hard to crack. His face had to be washed with waters mixed with many herbs, so that no evil eye would penetrate beyond his face to his heart. After all that, Okei was forced to drink a mixture which was supposed to get rid of any shyness he had.

The drink worked like a miracle. He started to sway to the drums of the Akpei people who were fast approaching the centre of the village. He laughed loudly when he heard the thin voices of Igbuno girls going to meet the new arrivals. People told him that Kwutelu and the others were singing his praises to the Akpei people, and this was annoying the girls who came with them. Okei then shouted: 'That is it. That is the spirit.'

They soon finished dressing him up and getting him emotionally ready. Then the drums all stopped as if on cue. Their places were taken by the biggest drum of all, that of the age-group dancers. This drum was beaten only once a year, at every yam festival season. It boomed, and its sound seemed to shake the very earth. Okei leapt into the air, and all the members of Agiliga's compound and all the members of the nearby compounds ran out, some carrying their locally made guitars, some carrying beer bottles and teaspoons to make music with. Children got empty tins and their covers. These musical instruments were all kept in secret before, waiting for the time they thought the spirit of the yam harvest and the coming of age would descend upon Okei. He led the crowd on, leaping and whirling in the air, until he neared the open place called Kumbi, where he knew that the Akpei contestants would be waiting. Someone had to stop him, because it was said that if he saw his opponent first he would not live to be an old man.

Four young men got hold of him and held him, forcing him to lean against the mud wall of Obi Uju's compound. Even Obi Uju, Kwutelu's father, came out and said prayers for Okei that he should bring glory to Igbuno.

All the other young Umu aya Biafra came and went into the square with their own relatives and friends, singing their praise-names and dancing with them. The other people, young members of the age-group, were slightly more sober than Okei. They too had been given the mixture, but not as strong as Okei's. Nduka too came with a big crowd. He was to take the place of Okei if he had an accident or got beaten. He was to be kept in reserve.

The Umu aya Biafra drum boomed from Obi Uju's compound, where the drummers had been hidden. The wordings of the drums were very clear: 'We will show you, we will show you.'

The farmer's boy from Ogbeukwu went into the circle and welcomed the people of Akpei, reminding them that it was he who had come to them to ask them for this match, a friendly one. He welcomed them again and showed them the pile of food and drinks which the parents of those coming of age had prepared. He introduced them to the girls who would be ready to get them anything they wanted. He then told them to choose a judge, and someone to act as a referee: the Igbuno boys had already chosen theirs. Whatever decisions these four people made would be final.

The Akpei spokesman, a young man of the same age-group, thanked the Igbuno people and hoped that after this kind of friendly match a greater bond of friendship would exist between the two villages.

The elders, Obi Agiliga, Obi Uju, and Obi Uwechue, and many others watched the proceedings from afar. They listened to the glowing speeches. One or two of them coughed a little and winked at the other. They all smiled and shook their heads knowingly.

14

The occasion started in a friendly way. The Igbuno dancers came and sang round the circle, they demonstrated their beautiful bodies and their agility. They were cheered and there was even great applause when girls performed acrobatic feats that took the breaths of the onlookers away. Josephine, Nduka's friend, was the leader of the acrobatic group. In acknowledging the cheers, they arranged themselves into such a pattern that they looked like the waters of Igbuno streams tumbling down the rocks into the valley beyond. The fact that the girls were not dressed in the latest abada cloth did not bother them. They came in tunics which they had made themselves. After the acrobatics, they threw loose lappas round themselves and danced their way out of the circle, followed by the great cheers of so many people.

There was hardly any living person left in Igbuno who was not at Kumbi that late afternoon. The sun was going down and it was nearing the cool of the evening. The cool breezes fanned the people from the surrounding coconut and oil palms.

The Akpei dancers were so well dressed that they could not move so quickly. People admired their outfits and hairdos, but their dance was nothing compared to the determined performance of the Igbuno girls. They did not receive so loud a cheer as the other group, and one could see frowns beginning to form themselves on the faces of the young men. Even some of the older women who came with them were murmuring behind the back of their hands. They were not given much time to grumble, because the big drum that was in Obi Uju's compound had been quietly moved nearer to the square. Then it boomed, so loud and so resonant that those people nearest to the drummers jumped and almost ran away from the circle. They quickly came back though, because they knew that if they did not they would lose their places. The crowd was ten to twelve people thick, like an impenetrable wall surrounding this circle.

As the drum boomed faster and faster Nduka jumped into the circle, ran fast round it, and dropped his cloak in the centre as a challenge to the Akpei people. The symbolic cloak was picked up by one of the referees. The drums beat even faster, and the circle was filled with all the boys of Igbuno born in and around the civil war. They had identical lappas, and their hair was cut in the same way. They were young, most of them slim and tall. They were proud and they showed it. Even the elders inched closer to admire the handsomeness of these young people who would take over the running of things when they were gone. They did a few light steps, and moved out of the circle.

Then the Akpei drummers took over, and their people were likewise shown. When the drums of the Igbuno people boomed again the four men holding Okei let him go. He danced into the square amidst the loudest cheer of that afternoon. He danced, and his young body pulsated in the cool of the evening. The Igbuno girls burst into song, praising him. His opponent watched him from his own side. Then at a sign from the referee, Okei threw his Akwete cloak on the ground and shouted: 'Come out, whoever you are.'

A young man, who was the same age as Okei but looked thicker and older somehow, leapt into the circle. And the wrestling started. The Akpei contestant kept looking for a way to pin down Okei, but he had been taught to wrestle like a dancer. He would leap here, run there, and dodge at the other place. They both sweated and panted, and Okei came closer only when he thought he had given his audience enough cheering and yelling for the afternoon. Okei was floored, almost at the very first close encounter. But he thanked his uncle in his heart. He used one of the surprise tactics he was taught, and his opponent was flat on the ground. He jumped on the boy from Akpei before he had time to recover from the shock, and held his arms in the air. Okei had won.

The excitement was terrific. The Igbuno people jumped and screamed in the air. But when the noise died down the Akpei people made it clear that an annual contest like that would not rest just on one wrestling match between two people only. They pushed in another boy, who floored Okei in no time at all. Arguments then started. The girls of Igbuno claimed that it was not fair for the Akpei people to have two contestants. So Nduka came in and the boy from Akpei floored him too. The Igbuno people became bitter and Okei could see that his people were becoming abusive, so he volunteered to wrestle with the same boy again. He did this, and he won.

Kwutelu was so excited that she jumped into the circle and started to wipe Okei's face with one of the handkerchiefs she was carrying. Then a shout came from one of the Akpei girls: 'Why don't you use that handkerchief to wipe your rubber ear!'

Nobody knew who hit the other person first, but every Igbuno boy found himself wrestling and fighting a boy from Akpei. The confusion became so intense that younger people screamed, as the adults called on the fighters to stop. But fists were in the air, and all the bottled anger of the past months was let loose.

'I think they will need us now,' said Obi Agiliga to the other Obis. They made their way into the confusion, and it took them a long time to disentangle the drumsticks from one of the drummers. They beat the drums as if they would bust, and shouted with their voices as well. Many of the fighters stopped unwillingly, as each was determined to get the better of the other.

Okei was grateful for the drums because two boys were really beating him without mercy. They asked him how he dared floor their best wrestlers. By the time the whole fight stopped blood was gushing down his nose, and both his feet felt like lead.

'This has been a very successful fight,' said Obi Agiliga. 'It has ended well . . . I mean the way we knew it would end. You have to stop punishing yourselves now. You all have to go home. We thank the girls for fanning the rumours and even taking part in fighting for their villages on this day. You can see for yourselves that you were all good wrestlers and fighters. And in all good fights, just like wars, nobody wins. You were all hurt and humiliated. I am sure you will always remember this day.'

'What is he talking about?' asked Kwutelu of Josephine, as she tried to tie her headscarf properly.

'He said that we should be thanked for fanning the rumours. But did we fan the rumours, Kwutelu? Did the elders use us to organize this wrestling match?'

'But why?' asked Kwutelu.

'Just to keep the boys busy. They were getting on everybody's nerves a few months ago. I think we have been used. What actually started the quarrel between us and the Akpei Umu Biafra?' asked Josephine.

'That's the trouble, I can't even remember.'

The two girls went back to their huts, very, very thoughtful.

Obi Agiliga and the other elders sat down to big kegs of palm-wine. 'It has all gone well, has it not?' Obi Uwechue asked.

The others nodded and drank a toast to the elders of any land.

'My nephew told me this morning that we would not be needed. If we had not appeared there on time, those Akpei boys would have torn him into pieces. I am glad they have got the message—in a good war, nobody wins.'